LITTLE APPLE GOAT

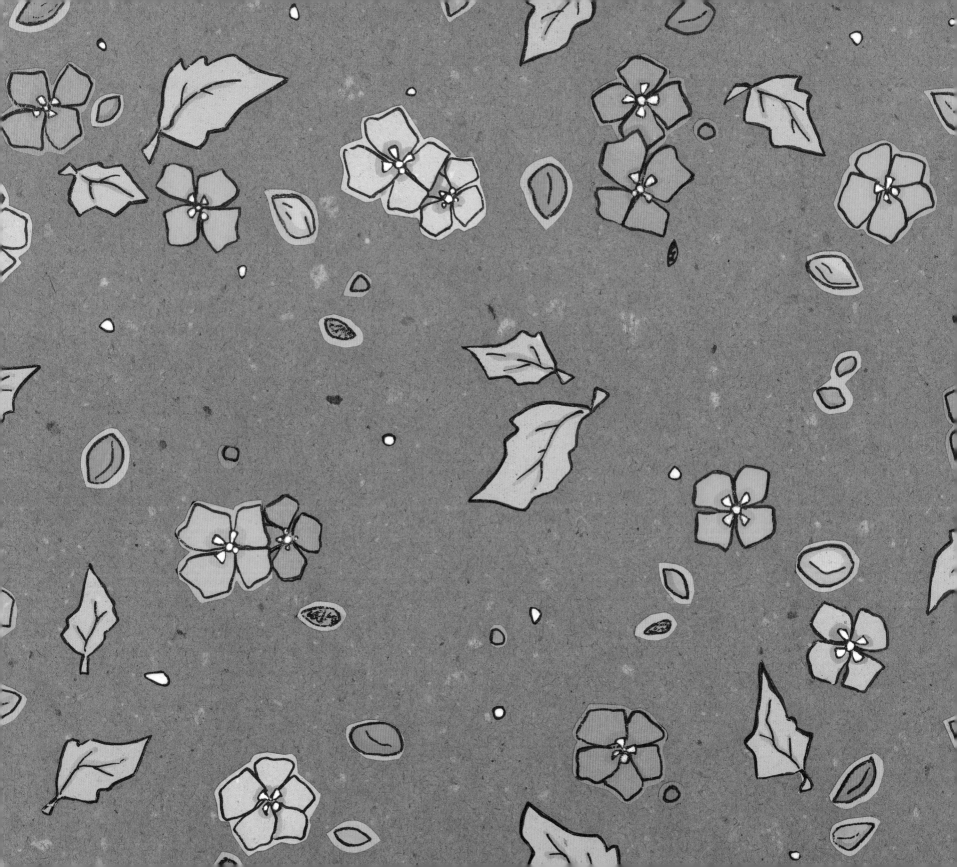

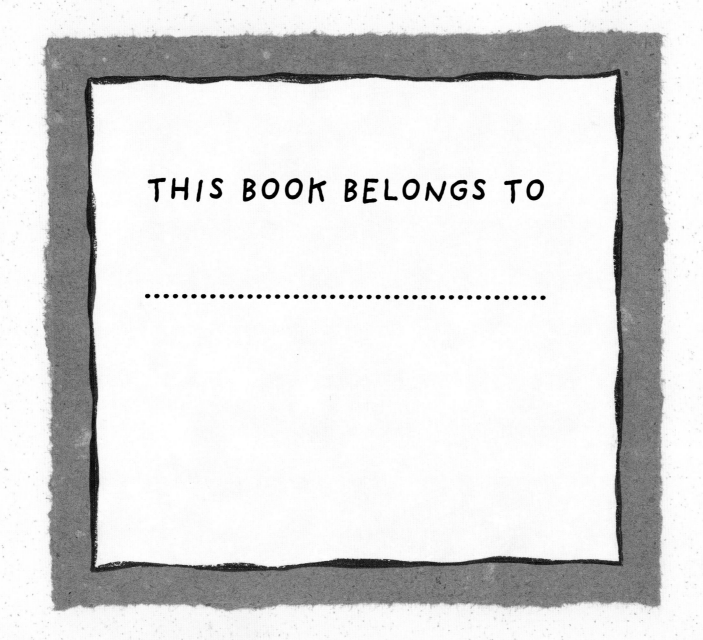

THIS BOOK BELONGS TO

....

For Siena, Oscar, Eleanor and Tegan

OXFORD
UNIVERSITY PRESS
Great Clarendon Street, Oxford OX2 6DP

Oxford University Press is a department of the University of Oxford.
It furthers the University's objective of excellence in research,
scholarship, and education by publishing worldwide in

Oxford New York
Auckland Cape Town Dar es Salaam Hong Kong Karachi
Kuala Lumpur Madrid Melbourne Mexico City Nairobi
New Delhi Shanghai Taipei Toronto

With offices in
Argentina Austria Brazil Chile Czech Republic France Greece
Guatemala Hungary Italy Japan Poland Portugal Singapore
South Korea Switzerland Thailand Turkey Ukraine Vietnam

Oxford is a registered trade mark of Oxford University Press
in the UK and in certain other countries

Database right Oxford University Press (maker)

First published 2007

British Library Cataloguing in Publication Data available

ISBN 978-019-279164-1 (hardback)
ISBN 978-019-279165-8 (paperback)

10 9 8 7 6 5 4 3 2 1

Printed in China

LITTLE
APPLE GOAT

Caroline Jayne Church

OXFORD

UNIVERSITY PRESS

Down on the farm
there lived a little goat.

She was quite an ordinary goat.
Ordinary in every way.
Every way, that is, except one.

She had most unusual eating habits.
While most goats are happy to chew
on last week's leftovers,

or Wednesday's washing,
Little Apple Goat preferred . . .

(She also loved cherries and pears.)

Every autumn, Little Apple Goat spent happy days in the orchard waiting for a crunchy apple, a juicy pear, or a ripe cherry to fall.

When evening came, Little Apple Goat trotted home to her meadow. And, on the way, she sent a shower of pips and stones over the hedge.

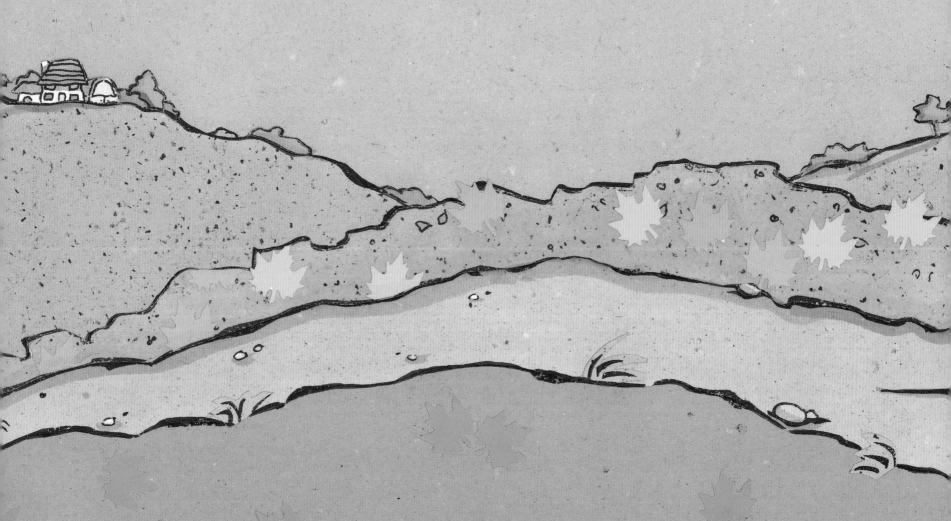

Plippety plip!

Day after day, year after year,
Little Apple Goat's pips and stones landed
in the top field, next to the hedge.

On one particular autumn day,
a breeze began to blow.

The breezy afternoon
became a blustery evening . . .

and the blustery evening
blew into a stormy night.

The animals were very scared indeed.
They huddled close together inside
the barn while the wind
howled all night long.

In the morning,
Little Apple Goat rushed
straight to the orchard.

The storm had toppled every single tree.
The orchard that Little Apple Goat loved
so much was gone.

All the animals were very sad when the farmer came to take the logs away.

'The farm just won't be the same again without the orchard,' they said.

As autumn turned to winter,
Little Apple Goat watched smoke
curl from the farmhouse chimney.

'At least the logs will keep
the farmer warm,' she thought.

At last spring came.

One day, as Little Apple Goat trotted
home to her meadow, she noticed some
young trees in the top field.
They were covered in blossom.

By the autumn the trees had grown bigger and the first fruits hung from their branches.

The farm had an orchard again!
'Hooray,' said the animals. 'But who could
have planted it?' they wondered.

Who indeed?

Plippety plip!